THE · BEAUTY · WHO WOULD · NOT · SPIN

By Adele Mongan Fasick

Illustrated by Leslie Elizabeth Watts

North Winds Press
A Division of Scholastic-TAB Publications Ltd., Richmond Hill, Ontario, Canada

This one is for Laura
A.M.F.

For my husband, Tony Luciani
L.E.W.

Art Director: Kathryn Cole

Text copyright © 1989 by Adele Mongan Fasick. Illustrations copyright © 1989 by Leslie Elizabeth Watts. All rights reserved.

No part of this publication may be reproduced or stored in a retrieval system, or transmitted in any form or by any means, electronic, mechanical, photocopying, recording, or otherwise, without written permission of the North Winds Press, 123 Newkirk Road, Richmond Hill, Ontario, Canada L4C 3G5

87654321   **Printed in Hong Kong**   9/801234/9

Canadian Cataloguing in Publication Data

Fasick, Adele M., 1930-
    The beauty who would not spin

Issued also in French under title: Celle qui ne voulait pas filer.
ISBN 0-590-71865-7

I. Watts, Leslie Elizabeth, 1961-   II. Title.

PS8561.A75B42 1989   jC813'.54   C88-093544-8
PZ7.F37Be 1989

Many years ago, in a small village in Ireland, there lived
a lovely young girl named Anastasia. Her family was poor
and her life hard, but Anastasia was cheerful and lively.
Everywhere she went she made friends. She loved to sing
and dance, and when she visited people she always left
them feeling happier than they were before.

But Anastasia had her faults. Although she worked willingly at other tasks, her mother despaired of ever teaching her to spin and weave and sew. When Anastasia sat down at the spinning wheel, her thread came out tangled and uneven. When she tried to weave, the cloth was crooked and lumpy. And she could scarcely thread a needle, much less sew a neat stitch.

Day after day Anastasia's mother would scold her, for she knew how important such skills were, especially for a poor family. But Anastasia paid no attention. After working only a few minutes at the spinning wheel, she would remember a sick neighbour and run off to the meadow to gather flowers for the woman's bedside table. She never seemed to worry.

One day as Anastasia was walking down the road toward the village, she saw two women. Both were tugging at a large bundle of flax.

"That's not fair," sputtered one of the women. "You are taking more than your share."

"It is too fair," answered the second. "Let's ask this girl."

They turned toward Anastasia, who was looking at them curiously. She thought she knew everyone who lived in the village, but she had never seen these women before. They were both wearing long grey dresses and had plaid shawls around their shoulders. The one who had just spoken had a very red nose. She smiled at Anastasia.

"Will you help us settle this quarrel?" she asked.

The second woman, who was shorter than the other and whose body was shaped like a jug, said, "Yes, please help us. Our aunt gave us this bundle of flax to divide between us. My sister insists on dividing the bundle because she is older than I am, but she is taking the larger portion for herself."

"I am doing it as evenly and carefully as I can," said the first woman, "so we will each have a fair share."

"Why don't you try it this way?" suggested Anastasia. "You divide the bundle, then let your younger sister choose which portion to take. If you have divided the flax evenly, you should both be satisfied."

The sisters agreed and the woman with the red nose carefully separated the flax into two bundles. When the other sister had chosen the bundle she wanted, they both thanked Anastasia kindly and went off down the road.

Anastasia continued toward the village. "I wish I could spend all my time helping people solve their problems," she thought. "It is much more fun than trying to spin and weave. I will never be able to do those things as well as my mother does. She will never be satisfied with me."

Anastasia had not gone very far when she saw another stranger sitting beside the road. Like the other two, this woman wore a long grey dress and a plaid shawl. She was crying softly.

"What is the matter?" asked Anastasia. "Are you hurt?"

"No," answered the woman. "I have been gathering flowers to decorate the house for my niece's wedding, but all the prettiest ones are on the other side of this fence and I cannot climb over it."

Anastasia looked down and saw that one of the woman's feet was much larger than the other. No wonder she could not climb the fence, with such a long foot to drag behind her.

"Let me help you," said Anastasia. Quickly she scaled the fence and jumped into the meadow on the other side. She gathered daisies, wild roses and tall larkspur for the woman, then nimbly climbed back over the fence.

Anastasia arranged the flowers into a beautiful bouquet and fastened it together with long stalks of grass. The woman thanked her and went happily off down the road.

"How can my fingers be so quick when I make a bouquet," thought Anastasia, "and so slow and clumsy when I thread a needle?"

A few days later, Prince Rowan rode through the village on his way from the castle. Just as he was passing the cottage door, Anastasia's mother was shouting in her loudest voice, "Stupid girl! Why don't you do as I tell you?"

The prince stopped his horse. "My good woman," he said, "why are you scolding this lovely girl?"

The mother did not want to criticize her daughter in front of the prince, so she quickly said, "Oh, Your Highness, I am scolding my daughter because I am worried that she works too hard. You may not believe this, but she spins three pounds of thread in one day, weaves it into cloth the next day, and makes five shirts on the third day."

"My mother will be happy to hear about that," said the prince. "Put your daughter up behind me on the horse and I will take her back to the castle. My mother insists that I marry, and if your daughter pleases her as much as she does me, she may become my bride. If she is willing, of course."

Anastasia's mother was so confused that she did not know what to do. But Anastasia was happy enough to climb up on the back of the horse and ride to the castle with the prince. She had always wondered what the castle was like.

As they rode over the fields and up the hill to the castle, the two young people talked about the things they liked to do. They never once mentioned spinning.

At first the queen was upset that her son was interested in a poor country girl. But when she heard how well Anastasia could spin and weave and sew, she decided that such a talented girl might be a good wife for her son after all.

Anastasia and the prince spent a cheerful evening together, talking and singing. Finally the queen, pleased to see the two of them so happy, led Anastasia to her bedroom.

"You see I have put a heap of fine flax in your room," she said. "I expect to see three pounds of thread by tomorrow."

Anastasia slept soundly and rose early to start her spinning. She had hoped the queen's flax might be easier to spin than the ordinary flax at home, but it was not. The thread would spin thin and fine one minute and then become lumpy. Anastasia stamped her foot in vexation.

Suddenly the door swung open and on the threshold stood the woman with the big foot. "Why are you so unhappy?" she asked.

"I will never be able to spin all the thread the queen expects," answered Anastasia, "and now that I know Prince Rowan I think I would like to marry him."

"If I spin the flax for you, will you invite me to your wedding?" asked the woman.

"You will be most welcome," Anastasia replied.

"Go off then and see your prince. I will spin the flax into thread."

So Anastasia and Prince Rowan spent a pleasant day wandering through the fields beyond the castle. He showed Anastasia how to bridle and saddle a horse, and she showed him how to find the freshest, sweetest mushrooms in the meadow.

When Anastasia returned to her room she found three pounds of fine strong thread on the floor beside the spinning wheel.

The queen was delighted. "What a dear girl you are," she said. "I shall have my own mahogany loom moved into your room. Tomorrow morning I shall expect to see some fine cloth."

Anastasia was even more worried about the weaving than she had been about the spinning. She had never learned to use the shuttle and scarcely knew how to begin. She was sitting sadly beside the loom when the jug-shaped woman appeared before her.

When she understood the reason for Anastasia's sorrow, the woman asked, "If I weave the cloth for you, will you invite me to your wedding?"

Anastasia gladly agreed, and in the morning she found a lovely cloth, fine and smooth as silk, lying beside the loom.

The queen smiled as she let the fine cloth run through her fingers. "Now," she said, "I will give you scissors and needles so you can sew this fine cloth into shirts."

Anastasia waited, expecting the third woman to appear. But an hour passed and she had not. Anastasia looked at the scissors, wondering how to begin. Finally the woman with the red nose appeared at the door.

She smiled in a kindly way. "I suppose you want me to do the cutting and sewing for you?" she asked.

"If you do not help me, the queen will not have any shirts," Anastasia admitted, "for I was never able to learn to sew."

"And you will invite me to your wedding?"

"Most gladly," answered the girl.

So the cutting and sewing was done that night while Anastasia slept. In the morning the queen came in and found five perfect shirts.

When Prince Rowan and Anastasia told the queen they would like to marry she readily agreed, and in no time at all a wedding was arranged. Anastasia's family and many friends attended the ceremony, but there was no sign of the three women who had helped her. She wondered why they had not come to the wedding after insisting that she invite them.

After the ceremony, all the guests were invited to a grand wedding feast. The queen told everyone about the excellent shirts Anastasia had made, and declared that after the honeymoon she and the bride would have a fine

time spinning, weaving and sewing together. Anastasia did not like the idea at all, nor was the prince any too happy to hear it. He did not want his bride occupied from morning till night, unable to ride with him.

He was about to say something to his mother when a footman appeared. "An old woman who says she is an aunt of the bride is waiting outside," he announced.

"Show her in," said Prince Rowan, "and give her a good place near the top of the table. All my bride's relatives are welcome."

When the woman with the big foot came in, the prince and the queen welcomed her kindly. But the queen could not keep from staring at the woman's foot. Finally she said, "May I ask what it is that makes your foot so big?"

"My foot has grown big because I spend all my time at the spinning wheel. I use that foot to push the treadle up and down."

When the prince heard this, he declared, "My wife shall never again spin thread."

A few minutes later the footman appeared again and announced that another aunt of the bride had arrived.

This time it was the jug-shaped woman, and again the queen could not contain her curiosity. "May I ask," she said, "why you are so wide halfway between the head and the feet?"

"I have grown this way because I spend all my days sitting at the loom," answered the woman.

"I don't want Anastasia to spend one more hour at the loom," said the prince. "Not one more hour."

It was not very long before the footman announced that yet another aunt had arrived. As Anastasia expected, it was the woman with the red nose.

In answer to the queen's question about the colour of her nose, the woman replied, "My nose has grown red because I spend so much of my time bent over my needle as I sew."

"Oh," gasped the prince, "my lovely bride shall never sew again. Instead of spending her time bending over needle-work, she shall ride with me throughout the kingdom and learn more about our people."

27

And that is just what happened. The people learned
to love Anastasia and Prince Rowan. Anastasia was often
asked to settle quarrels, and she always settled them fairly
and kindly. She and the prince worried about the problems
rulers must worry about and made better laws than the
country had ever known.

Nor did the queen mind. The three women visited the castle often. They were full of wonderful tales, which they told as they all worked with flying fingers at their spinning, weaving and sewing.

It may be that the queen suspected Anastasia was not so
fond of needlework after all, and that the three women had
something to do with the five beautiful shirts. But if she did,
she never said anything. And they all lived in happy
harmony for many years.